# MR. MEN
## go Swimming

Roger Hargreaves

D0549872

Hello, my name is Walter. Can you spot me in this book?

EGMONT

There are lots of places that you can go swimming.

You can swim in the sea.

You can swim in the river.

But you cannot swim in the bath!

Mr Tickle decided to learn to swim in a swimming pool.

He arrived at the pool and went into the changing rooms.

Mr Dizzy was there for a swim, but being Mr Dizzy he was putting on a scarf and gloves.

He had been told that the water was a bit cold.

Silly old Mr Dizzy!

As you know, Mr Tickle has extraordinarily long arms.

And it turned out that extraordinarily long arms do not make swimming easy.

First of all he tried breaststroke.

Then Mr Clever showed him front crawl.

And Little Miss Wise suggested backstroke.

But for all Mr Tickle's attempts he could not learn to swim.

So Mr Tickle decided to sit and watch everybody else to see what he could learn.

He watched Mr Rush surging up and down the pool.

He watched Little Miss Naughty bombing
Little Miss Tiny.

And he watched Little Miss Somersault diving from the high board.

Of course, Mr Tickle being Mr Tickle, he could not just sit and watch.

He could not resist a tickle or two.

He tickled Little Miss Splendid off her lilo.

He tickled Little Miss Shy to the surface.

And he tickled Mr Worry into the pool!

But how was he going to learn to swim?

And then he had an idea.

Armbands!

But not just two armbands.

Oh no, not with arms as long as Mr Tickle's.

Mr Tickle needed three armbands for each arm!

Which were very helpful for swimming.

But absolutely no good for tickling.

The armbands kept getting in the way!